# Beast Quest®

# ST...
# THE LURKING TERROR

## BY ADAM BLADE

# With special thanks to Tabitha Jones

## *For Bee Walters*

www.beastquest.co.uk

ORCHARD BOOKS

First published in Great Britain in 2022 by The Watts Publishing Group

1 3 5 7 9 10 8 6 4 2

Text © Beast Quest Limited 2022
Cover and inside illustrations by Steve Sims
© Beast Quest Limited 2022

Beast Quest is a registered trademark of Beast Quest Limited
Series created by Beast Quest Limited, London

A CIP catalogue record for this book is available from the British Library.

ISBN 978 1 40836 538 0

Printed in Great Britain

The paper and board used in this book are made from wood from responsible sources

Orchard Books
An imprint of Hachette Children's Group
Part of The Watts Publishing Group Limited
Carmelite House, 50 Victoria Embankment, London EC4Y 0DZ

An Hachette UK Company
www.hachette.co.uk
www.hachettechildrens.co.uk

# Welcome to the world of Beast Quest!

Tom was once an ordinary village boy, until he travelled to the City, met King Hugo and discovered his destiny. Now he is the Master of the Beasts, sworn to defend Avantia and its people against Evil. Tom draws on the might of the magical Golden Armour, and is protected by powerful tokens granted to him by the Good Beasts of Avantia. Together with his loyal companion Elenna, Tom is always ready to visit new lands and tackle the enemies of the realm.

While there's blood in his veins, Tom will never give up the Quest…

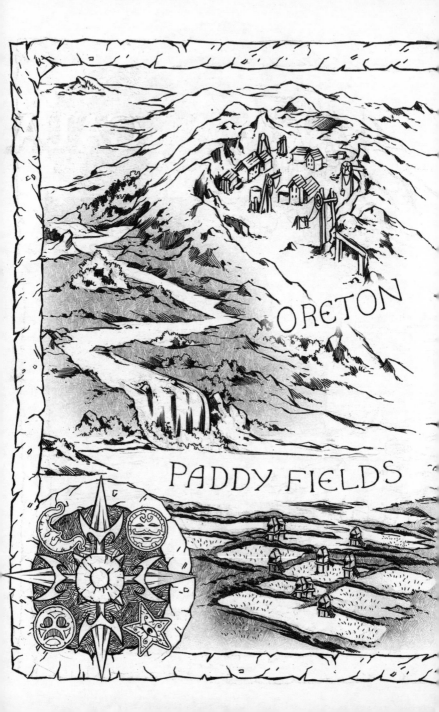

ORETON

PADDY FIELDS

There are special gold coins to collect in this book. You will earn one coin for every chapter you read.

Find out what to do with your coins at the end of the book.

# CONTENTS

*You thought I was gone, did you not? Swallowed by the Netherworld, never to set foot in the upper world again... Consumed by the Beasts that roam this foul place... Well, it's not that easy to be rid of the most powerful magician who ever stalked the land.*

*I have the perfect plan up my sleeve, and soon I shall leave this Realm of Beasts behind.*

*And the best part? My arch enemy Tom will die in the process.*

*See you all very soon!*

*Malvel*

# THE DARKEST NIGHT

Tom drew the last fragment of bread from the pouch at his belt. It was stale, and so small it would barely take the edge off his hunger. Still, he took a small bite, washing it down with a sip from his flask. He had to tip the waterskin right back to reach the gritty dregs at the bottom.

"I'm almost out of water," Tom told Elenna. She sat opposite him, her knees drawn up under her chin, hugging herself to keep warm.

"My flask's almost empty too," she said, through chattering teeth. "We'll need to find more soon. And I wish we had wood for a campfire. Or even a branch to make a torch. It's so cold!"

Tom rubbed at his arms and legs, trying to shift the bone-aching chill that had leached into them while he slept on the rocky ground. Beyond Elenna, he could see nothing but blackness. They had stopped only briefly to recover from their battle with the jackal-Beast, Ossiron. In that short time, night had fallen in the Netherworld, turning the air bitterly cold.

"We'll warm up as soon as we start moving again," Tom said, drawing a map from inside his tunic. With no moon or stars, it was their only way of navigating through the strange, gloomy realm. Unfortunately, the map had a voice and a mind of its own – that of Zarlo. *Can we really trust a wizard careless enough to get stuck inside his own map?* Tom wondered. Then he sighed. They had little choice.

"Still not given up, then?" Zarlo asked chirpily as Tom unfurled the parchment.

"You know we can't do that," Tom said. "Not while three more innocent lives depend on us." Tom and Elenna were on a Quest to rescue four young candidates for the title of Tangala's new Master of the Beasts. They had been kidnapped by Malvel, Tom's oldest enemy. The Evil Wizard had transported the contestants to the Netherworld, hoping to bargain their lives for his freedom. Tom and Elenna had already rescued a brave lad called Nolan, but three other young hopefuls remained lost in the realm, guarded by Beasts.

"So you keep saying," Zarlo said. "But something's been bothering me. Surely this wizard, Marvin or

Malvin or
whatever his
name is, can't
really be that
dangerous.
I've never
even heard of
him."

Tom
frowned,
baffled. *Everyone's heard of Malvel!
How long has Zarlo been trapped in
this map?*

"Believe me," Tom said, "he's
dangerous. He's probably the most
powerful wizard ever to have lived."

Zarlo sniffed. "He got trapped
here in the Netherworld, didn't he? I

didn't have any problems travelling here at all."

"Hmm," Elenna said. "Apart from the one slight problem of getting yourself stuck inside a map. How did that happen again?"

"Bah! Not through lack of power, I can assure you," Zarlo said. "It was a simple mistake in the words of a spell. A mispronunciation, if you like. Could have happened to anyone. Now, do you want some help or are you just going to ask foolish questions? I seem to recall you said something about fire..."

Before Tom could argue, Zarlo muttered a few strange, guttural words, and a green fire sizzled into life on the ground between Tom and Elenna. Flames licked up towards Zarlo's map, singeing the edges. Tom whipped the parchment out of the way before it caught light.

"Oops! Bit of a close one there!" Zarlo said. "That's the trouble with being so powerful. It's a risky business. Which is why I can assure you, Malvel can't possibly be as powerful as I am…or…er…was…"

"You might be right," Tom said, knowing it was best to keep the wizard happy. "But Malvel's got a book of spells that you must have heard of. The *Book of Derthsin*?"

"Derthsin? The name does ring a bell," said Zarlo thoughtfully.

"Remind me."

Tom took a deep breath, doing his best to stay patient though he was desperate to get moving. "Derthsin was an ancient Evil sorcerer who controlled Beasts with magic. He could also change the landscape around him – turn air to fire, earth to water, raise mountains from plains, change jungle to desert. Now that Malvel has Derthsin's book, he'll be able to use all these powerful spells."

"Interesting," Zarlo muttered. "Very interesting..."

Frustration welled inside Tom but before he could snap at Zarlo, Elenna grabbed his arm, pointing to the starless sky. "Look!" Tom saw a darker blot of black sweep overhead, then heard a high, thin screech. Another shadowy form flitted past, then another.

Elenna shuddered, rubbing at the deep cuts that scored her arms. "Janus birds!" she said. Tom couldn't blame her for being afraid. The horrible creatures had already attacked her once, rending her flesh with their sharp beaks and talons.

"Malvel's spies," Tom said. "They must have spotted our fire. Zarlo – can you put it out?"

Zarlo snorted and muttered something about ingratitude, but the flames of his fire quickly died. "That's your nearest Beast," Zarlo said, as a glowing purple spot appeared on the map in Tom's hands. "But don't say I didn't warn you. Styx lives in a stinking swamp. He's bad-tempered at the best of times and always hungry. You'd be much better off going home."

"Not while there's blood in my veins," Tom said.

Zarlo cackled. "Thought you might say that! Completely bonkers, the pair of you."

Tom looked at Elenna and saw her features were set with the same firm resolve he felt. "Let's get going," he said. "The lives of three brave young Tangalans depend on us."

# THE POISONED VALLEY

By day, Tom had found the Netherworld a forlorn and desolate place. By night, it was a thousand times worse. The darkness was so complete Tom could barely see his hand held out before his face, and a strange stifling silence muffled even the sound of his own steps. He and

Elenna trekked through the starless night, stamping their feet and blowing on their hands to stop them from freezing, trying to close the gap between themselves and the glowing spot on the map.

But finally, the faintest tinge of dawn crept into the inky sky. To Tom's relief it got steadily warmer. Eventually, he began to make out the ragged outline of what looked like thick bushes ahead.

"Do you think that's the swamp?" Elenna asked.

"It looks like it," said Tom, glancing at the map.

"Still time to turn back if you want," Zarlo added.

Tom pretended not to hear. He quickened his stride and soon they neared the line of dense vegetation. The ground dropped sharply away, forcing them to stop. Tom could see that what he had taken for bushes were actually trees growing in a steep-sided valley. Ancient knobbly trunks stood in uneven ranks all the way to the valley floor, their wide branches and dark leaves jostling for space. Tangled curtains of hairy vine hung from every bough and immense ferns smothered the ground. Uneasy shivers tingled up and down Tom's spine as he surveyed the undergrowth.

Something was nagging at him...

"It's too quiet," Elenna said.

*That's what it is!* There should have been birdsong, or at least the buzz of insects. But everything was eerily silent. Tom looked again at the map, then frowned. He couldn't see the marker for the Beast any more. As he searched for it, the spot reappeared, then vanished again.

Tom growled with frustration. "The Beast's down there somewhere," he said. "But it keeps disappearing."

"Don't worry," Zarlo said. "Even if you can't find Styx, I'm sure that he'll find you."

"Very reassuring," Elenna said.

Tom tucked the map into his tunic
to free his hands for the climb and
started to edge his way down the
slope. Though he turned sideways
for a better
grip, his
boots slipped
almost
instantly,
sending loose
stones and
soil tumbling
away ahead
of him. Tom
grabbed a
thick vine
to steady
himself. He started off again,

treading more carefully than ever. Elenna followed close behind him, and together they picked their way down the valley side.

Tom scanned the shadows all around them as they went, listening out for any sign of the Beast. He began to notice a soft rustling sound – so quiet he almost thought he was imagining it at first. It seemed to come from every direction at once. *Just the breeze in the leaves*, he told himself. But the air was ominously still.

As the strange purple light of the Netherworld day brightened, a fine mist rose up from the loamy ground. With it came the sweet scent of flowers. The rustling noise grew louder and, glancing at the branches all around him, Tom realised with a jolt of amazement what was making the sound. *It's the plants!* Glossy green buds were opening right before his eyes, revealing brightly coloured petals inside.

"Look!" Elenna said, pointing at a trumpet-shaped orange blossom as it unfurled. "How pretty!" Another flower unfolded beside it, this one shaped like a pink butterfly. "And what a wonderful smell!" Elenna said. "Perhaps this place isn't so bad after all."

Tom smiled and nodded, but as he looked from the plant to Elenna, then back again, his vision blurred. He could see two of everything. Tom blinked and rubbed his eyes, but that made the blurring worse. And now black spots were filling his vision, growing together, blocking his sight.

"Tom, what's happening?" Elenna said, her voice sharp with panic. "I can't see properly." Tom felt her grab his arm, but he couldn't see her at all. He couldn't see anything.

He took a deep breath. "We need to stay calm," he said. "It started when the flowers opened, so let's move away from them. Then hopefully our vision will come back."

"But how do we know which way

to go if we can't see?" Elenna asked.

"We'll just have to keep heading downwards," Tom said. "Take my hand so we don't lose each other." Elenna shifted her grip from his arm, her palm cool and firm as she grasped his hand.

Tom eased himself slowly down the slope, drawing Elenna with him. Using his free hand to guide them from branch to branch, he slid his feet over the treacherous ground. Soft, spidery things brushed against his face, making his skin crawl. Twigs and roots clawed at his legs. Tom skidded suddenly, his stomach lurching as he fell. He landed hard on his back and somehow managed to grab a tuft of fern to stop himself, but not before he'd scraped his spine and lost his grip on Elenna's hand.

"Zarlo! Can you guide us?" Tom asked, drawing out the map. "We can't see."

"You know, I'd almost forgotten about those flowers," Zarlo said, so calmly Tom felt his temper flare. "Their pollen's terrible stuff for the eyes," Zarlo went on. "Very disorientating. If I remember rightly, there's water nearby. If you keep going down, just a little further, you can wash the pollen away."

"Thank you," Tom said, trying to keep the irritation from his voice.

"And maybe if you remember anything else like that, you could let us know?" Elenna snapped. Then she let out a sharp yelp. "Tom, was that you?" she asked. "Did you grab me?"

"No?" Tom said. As he spoke, something snatched his own wrist – something strong, dry and hairy. Tom's skin crawled. *It feels like...a vine?*

Tom yanked his arm free. "It's the plants!" he told Elenna, feeling another loop of vegetation catch at his leg. "They're attacking. We have to get out of here!" Tom kicked and tore himself free of the vine, then skidded faster down the slope. He hands tore blindly at foliage to try to slow himself. The moving vines snagged his arms and grabbed clumps of his hair, throwing him off balance. He dashed them away.

"Elenna?" he called as he struggled onwards. "Are you all right?"

"I'm just behind you," she replied. "I'll meet you at the bottom."

Tom half-tumbled on down the slope, grazing his elbows and skinning his palms. Thorns cut into his skin. He kept going, wrenching himself free of the clutching vines, until finally he felt sticky mud suck at his boots. He caught an eggy taint of swamp water in the air. Cool water welled up around his ankles. Tom bent down and scooped the water into his eyes, washing away the pollen that had made him blind. Soon he could see blotches of light and colour. He blinked. The outline of bushes and trees came into focus. Relief flooded Tom's chest. *I can see!* But then he turned around to look for Elenna. All he could see was hanging creepers and bushy ferns. His heart gave a painful leap. *She's gone!*

# KATYA'S AXE

"Elenna!" Tom shouted, scrambling back the way he had come, crashing through the ferns and creepers that seemed to have closed up behind him. "Where are you?" Tom paused for a moment to listen but could only hear the hideous rustling creak of the moving vines. It sounded almost like poisonous laughter. Drawing his sword, Tom slashed at branches, chopping off groping lengths of vine, smashing his way through.

"Elenna!" he called again. This time he heard a muffled cry from up ahead. It was Elenna's voice, but strangled and terrified. Tom clawed up the steep, slippery slope, hacking everywhere with his sword. Finally, he pushed through into a small clearing. Now he could hear Elenna's muffled cries clearly but he still couldn't see her.

Then he looked up and gasped. Elenna was hanging face-down from a gnarled branch. Thick vines

were looped
around
her ankles
and wrists,
holding her
in place.
Another
length
of mossy
creeper had
snaked its

way around her face, covering her
mouth completely. Her eyes were
wide and round, and though she was
looking straight at Tom, they didn't
register him at all. *She still can't see
me!*

"I'm coming!" Tom called.

Sheathing his sword, he launched himself on to the trunk of the tree Elenna was hanging from and began to shimmy upwards. The bark was strangely spongy and peeled away in strips under Tom's hands like scabs from a wound, but he dug his nails in deep and kept going. He clambered on to the lowest bough, leaping between branches. Elenna's face twisted with pain. The vines had tightened. Blood trickled down her wrists and ankles.

"I'm almost with you!" Tom hauled himself on to the branch below her and drew his sword.

"I'm going to cut your arm free first," he told Elenna. "You can take my hand, and then I'll cut the rest of the vines." Elenna nodded mutely, her eyes clamped shut in pain. Tom chopped away the first vine. Elenna grabbed for him blindly, catching hold of his hand in a vice-like grip. With another slash, he severed the vine that covered her mouth. Elenna gasped with relief. Next, Tom freed her left leg, then her right, guiding her body on to his branch with his arms as she dropped towards him. Finally, he chopped through the last tendril holding her wrist.

"Can you grip on to me?" Tom asked Elenna. "I have to get us down from here."

Elenna wrapped her arms firmly around his neck and clung on.

Calling on the enhanced strength of his golden breastplate Tom

 grabbed hold of a thick vine, and slid down to the ground, carrying Elenna with him.

"Come with me," he said, setting Elenna down and taking hold of her hand. Still blind and breathless, Elenna nodded.

"I trust you," she said.

Tom used his sword to slash a

new path as he quickly led her back to the muddy pool where he had washed his face. "Scoop up some water to clean the pollen away from your eyes."

Elenna knelt and splashed water on to her face, then she blinked the mud from her eyes. "I really don't like this place! Zarlo, maybe next time you could warn us about sheer drops, poisonous pollen and strangling vines…"

"I can't be expected to remember everything," the wizard said as Tom pulled out the map. "You'd be forgetful too if you knew as much as I do."

Tom clenched his jaw. "Just tell

me, is there anything else we should know?"

"Indeed there is," Zarlo said. "You have just washed your faces in Styx's swamp. There is a good chance he knows that you're here now, so better not go for a swim."

"Very helpful!" Elenna said.

The small purple dot was pulsing on the map. Suddenly, it vanished. "What does it mean when the Beast's mark disappears?" Tom asked Zarlo.

"Obviously, it means I'm not sure where Styx is," the wizard answered. "But as I said, you'll find him soon enough."

Elenna glared at the map for a

moment. Then, with a shake of her head, she turned her attention to the swamp. Tom did the same. He was suddenly glad he hadn't been able to see the water while he washed his face in it. It was muddy and covered in algae.

Tom led the way as they skirted carefully around the edge of the pool. The swamp was so thick with murk it could have been any depth. Yellow foam sat in frothy clumps on the surface and occasional bubbles rose from the depths, sending out concentric ripples, as if something was slithering around underneath. The eggy stench of rotting vegetation was almost overpowering.

Trees rose from the putrid water and stood along its banks, but they all seemed to have died long ago. Blackened branches hung from them at crazy angles, and tidelines of black slime ran around their decaying trunks. Jagged holes yawned in the rotting wood like gaping mouths. Even the vines that hung from the trees were black and dead.

The mud squelched and sucked at Tom's boots as he walked, sending up more bursts of rank-smelling fumes. Elenna suddenly gave a yelp and almost tripped as her boot hit something hidden in the sludge. She bent and prised it free.

"Oh no," Elenna murmured, holding up a hefty metal axe. Tom's stomach sank as he recognised it.

"Katya's axe," he said. "We're too late."

"Not necessarily," Elenna said. "Maybe she's trapped, like I was." Tom glanced again at the map he held. Among the trees at the bottom of the valley he could see a large, rough oval marking the shape of the swamp, with smaller islands inside it. The dull spot that marked the Beast had reappeared and was more or less in the middle.

"She might be trapped on one of those islands," Tom said. "We should build a raft and look for her."

Elenna nodded. With so much dead wood lying around, it didn't take long to make a structure big enough to carry them both. Tom used Katya's axe to chop the least rotten branches they could find and bound them together with lengths of vine.

As soon as the raft was finished, Tom stepped aboard, taking a long twigless branch with him to use as a punt pole. Foetid brown water oozed up beneath his feet, but the vessel held. Once Elenna had climbed on beside him, Tom shoved off from the shore.

Standing with his legs braced wide, Tom pushed the raft through

the murky
water, easing
it between
muddy
banks and
clumps
of dank
vegetation.
Each time
he shoved
off with his

pole, it sank deep into thick, sticky
sludge, and when he pulled it free,
bubbles rose, releasing bursts of
vile gas. Rotting branches arched
together overhead, casting dark
reflections on the water. Slimy weed
hung from the matted tangle of vine

that draped the trees. Elenna knelt in the centre of the raft, peering into the gloom all around them, an arrow ready in her bow. Tom ran his gaze over the surface of the water, looking for anything moving...anything alive.

Suddenly Tom heard a soft splash, followed by a plop from somewhere up ahead. Elenna aimed, narrowing her eyes...

*Thud!* A heavy weight landed on the raft behind Tom, making it buck. Before he could turn, a strong hand slapped over his mouth, clamping it shut, and something cold and sharp was pressed against his throat as a young voice hissed in his ear.

"Don't move, or you're dead!"

# THE LURKING
# TERROR ATTACKS

Tom stood as still as he could on the bobbing raft. The blade – or whatever it was – dug painfully into his throat.

"Let him go, or I'll shoot!" Elenna exclaimed, the raft tipping slightly as she shifted her stance.

"He'll be dead before you kill

me!" Tom's captor hissed. Her voice was young, but full of command – and familiar.

"Katya?" Elenna said, suddenly.

"Yeees?" the young voice answered tentatively. Then, "Oh!" Tom suddenly felt the point at his throat recede and the hand drop from his mouth. "It's you!" the girl said.

Tom turned. A tall girl with a fierce look in her brown eyes stood before him. He had last seen her tumbling through a portal in Pania. *It is Katya!* Relief washed over Tom to see her alive.

"Tom, Elenna," Katya went on, glancing between them. "I'm so sorry! I didn't recognise you... You look…awful." Katya's hair fell in tangles around her face, which was smeared with mud. Every part of her clothing seemed to be dirty or torn, and she was only wearing one boot.

"You don't look so great yourself," Elenna said, smiling wryly. "But I'm glad we found you in one piece. When we came across your axe, we feared the worst!"

Katya grinned,

shoving her makeshift flint blade
into her belt as Elenna handed her
the axe. "I can't believe you came
to rescue me!" Katya said. "To start
with, I thought this was a part of the
trial – a test I had to get through.
But when no one came, I figured
I was on my own." Katya lowered
her voice and put a finger to her
lips. "Although not *quite* alone," she
whispered. "There's a Beast in this
swamp. It's got good hearing, and
very good camouflage."

"Styx?" Tom asked.

Katya nodded. "If that's the name
of the giant alligator thing that
almost bit my leg off. When I fell
through that portal, I landed in

the mud at the edge of this swamp. Before I could even work out what had happened, this great brute of an alligator yanked me into the water by my leg." Katya shuddered. "I would have died down there, but my boot came loose in its mouth, and I swam for it. I've been keeping out of its reach ever since, staying in the trees mostly. But the Beast's hard to keep track of. You'd hardly know it was there, until it's too late."

"We should be able to find out more or less where the Beast is," Tom said, drawing out the map.

"Yes, you will. In fact, here he is now. Hello, Styx!" Zarlo said.

"There!" Elenna said, gesturing to a

series of broad, arrow-shaped ripples in the swamp. Something was gliding towards them beneath the surface. Something huge!

Tom plunged his pole deep into the swamp, propelling the raft away from the Beast, just as Styx's huge, scaled head burst from the water. Tom saw cold reptilian eyes and an enormous maw crammed with sharp teeth, before the Beast seemed to blur, then vanish. *SNAP!* Tom's pole exploded, bitten clean in half.

Tom looked for the Beast, but saw only swirling water — then, *CHOMP!* The raft bucked and Styx reappeared with his powerful jaws clamped around half of the raft. Styx

thrashed his head from side to side,
making the vessel pitch and roll.

Katya slammed into Tom, almost
throwing him from the raft, but
Elenna yanked him back. Dropping
into a crouch, Tom raised his sword

to strike the Beast, but Styx's outline blurred once more.

Elenna's arrow whizzed past Tom, lodging in something with a *thwack*, and the Beast became clearly visible – scarred, armoured hide, glassy yellow eyes. He shook his mighty head, dislodging the arrow from his scales, and vanished. Tom frowned, scanning the murky water... *CRASH!* The raft leapt as their invisible enemy latched on to it again.

All Tom could see was churning muddy water and splintering wood, but he sent his sword whistling down. *CRACK!* It slammed into Styx's invisible skull and bounced off. Tom saw the Beast for a moment as Styx let go of the raft, a new gash visible on his armoured snout. But then Styx dipped below the choppy water.

"We have to get out of the swamp!" Tom cried, hacking a low-hanging branch from a tree. Using it as a pole, he pushed them through the swamp as fast as he could.

Katya quickly grabbed another branch to help, while Elenna aimed an arrow towards the place where Styx had vanished. Glancing back, Tom could already see the Beast's tell-tale ripples angling towards them. But the raft had almost reached the shore. Using all his remaining strength, Tom gave an enormous shove, grounding the raft on the muddy bank.

"GO!" he told Katya. She leapt, landing well clear of the water. Elenna sent a final arrow slicing across the swamp towards the Beast as Tom jumped ashore.

"Quick!" Tom called to Elenna, turning. Elenna bent her knees to leap – but at the same moment, the raft exploded into shards behind her as Styx's giant snout burst through it, flinging her towards Tom. He reached out to catch her, but suddenly, her expression changed to a look of alarm. Tom saw that Styx's jagged teeth had caught the fabric of her tunic. Time seemed to slow, and Tom watched in horror as his friend was snatched away from him, disappearing under the water so fast she didn't even have time to scream.

# 5

# GONE

Tom stared at the spot where Elenna
had vanished, ready to leap in after
his friend, but the swamp was
totally still with no trace of Elenna
or the Beast. Tom snatched the map
from his tunic and unrolled it. He
couldn't see the Beast's purple dot
anywhere.

"Where are they, Zarlo?" Tom

demanded desperately.

"I'm afraid that the Beast is currently too well camouflaged for me to find," Zarlo said.

"But what about Elenna?"

"I have no way of tracing her."

Tom shoved the map back into his tunic. He ignored the wizard's muffled protests and paced the shore, frustration and horror burning in his chest.

"She might be all right," Katya said. "Elenna's fought so many Beasts, and I managed to get away from him."

Tom spun to face the girl, guilt and anguish making him fierce. "You escaped because Malvel wanted you alive. He used you as bait to get to me. Elenna won't be so lucky!"

Katya stared at him open-mouthed for a moment. Then she frowned. "If the Beast is trying to lure you, that means Elenna is still alive."

Tom rubbed at his face with his hands. He felt sick and cold. He looked at Katya, with her one muddy boot. He made a decision. "At least I can get you to safety," Tom said, taking the purple jewel from his belt. "I'm going to open a portal to the palace so that I can send you home."

"No way!" Katya said, holding up her hands. "I've been observing this Beast for a while now. I can help you. We need to get out there and look for Elenna."

"That's what I intend to do as soon as you're safe," Tom said. "I don't have time to argue."

"You can't send me anywhere against my will," Katya said. "I'm going to look for Elenna. You can stay here if you want." Katya turned to their raft. It was only half the size it had been before, but still floating.

"No!" Tom cried. "It's too dangerous!" But then he heard a distant shout.

"Tom!" It was Elenna's voice, muffled and faint, but definitely her.

"See?" Katya said. "Now let's go and find her." Katya cupped her hands to her mouth and called out over the swamp. "We're coming, Elenna!"

Tom put his purple jewel back into his belt. Now the numb shock of losing Elenna was receding, he felt the heat of shame flood to his face. "I'm sorry for shouting," he told Katya. "You were right. Let's go!"

With Tom and Katya both pushing the raft along, they made swift progress through the still, muddy waters. Tom checked the map often, but the Beast did not reappear. They followed the sound of Elenna's voice until they spotted a tiny island through the mist. A single crooked tree stood in the middle of it, draped in loops of twisted vine. Elenna was clinging to one of the tree's bare, rotting branches. She was soaked to the skin and covered in mud and green slime, but Tom had never been more pleased to see her.

Elenna leapt down as they reached the island and helped them

pull the raft ashore.

"How did you escape?" Katya asked Elenna.

"Once Styx had me under the water he went into a roll," Elenna said. "I think he was trying to drown me. I couldn't see anything, but I grabbed on to his scales, and used an arrow as a dagger. I must have got lucky. I stabbed him right in the eye. He went crazy, thrashing around, and his camouflage failed for a moment." Elenna stopped to swallow, her face very pale under the grime. "Tom – Styx is huge and made completely of muscle. His scales are like stone and his eyes…" She shuddered. "They are so cold and alien. It's like he wasn't seeing me as a living thing at all. Just as food. Anyway, I swam away as fast as I could and got out of the water."

Tom nodded. Elenna's words confirmed something he had already noticed. Styx wasn't like other Beasts. There was something far more ancient about him. Primeval, almost. *And there was something odd about the way he attacked our raft too...*

"I have an idea," Tom said. "From below the surface, I don't think Styx has any way of knowing whether we're on the raft or not. If we stay here and send the raft out as a distraction, we can ambush him when he attacks."

"But then we're stranded in the middle of a Beast-infested swamp with no way to get out," Katya said.

"We either send the raft out as a distraction, or we go ourselves," Tom said. "We don't have any other option."

"He's right," Elenna said.

Katya looked uneasy, but then smiled and nodded, tossing her axe from hand to hand. "Let's do it," she said.

Tom gave the raft a hefty shove, pushing it out into the swamp, then drew Zarlo's map from inside his tunic. Almost at once, he saw the faint purple spot that marked the Beast's location appear – and it was moving, slowly to start with but picking up pace, towards the point where their raft had stopped.

"It's working," Tom said. "Be ready."

1

# 6

# AMBUSH

Tom, Elenna and Katya all focussed on the raft floating silently on the stagnant brown water. Tom noticed a faint current swirling around the edges of the vessel. *BOOM!* The raft burst apart, splintered wood flying in every direction as the muddy water splashed and foamed. Elenna loosed an arrow.

*THUNK!* The missile appeared to stop in mid-flight above the churning waves. The air shimmered and Styx became visible, Elenna's arrow protruding from his armoured hide. Tom stared in horrified awe. The Beast continued to worry at the remains of their raft, completely ignoring the arrow in his flank. His enormous body was equal in size to a mighty beech or elm, and his scarred and pitted scales looked far tougher than any bark. Styx's thick, muscular tail whipped from side to side as he snapped at the last fragments of wood. His colossal jaws lined with pointed teeth were easily big enough to swallow a person whole.

Looking into the Beast's stony reptilian eyes, Tom put a hand to the red jewel in his belt.

*You must yield*, he told Styx. *Renounce your new Master, Malvel, and we shall leave you in peace.*

*No, small human! You are in my swamp, which makes you fair hunting game.* Styx's voice in Tom's mind was a low, hungry growl.

*Then I shall have to defeat you!* Tom told the Beast. He bent his knees and leapt, landing astride Styx's broad back just as the alligator-Beast vanished again. But, gripping the Beast's solid, muscular form, Tom didn't need to rely on sight. He hacked at the Beast's hide with all his strength. *CLANG!* Tom's blade ricocheted off, sending a jolt of pain up his arm. Styx bucked and writhed, but Tom held fast with his legs and chopped again. It was like striking plate armour. Tom's arm rang with the force of his blows, but Styx barely seemed to register them. *This is hopeless!* Elenna fired another arrow, but it too clattered off Styx's scales.

Tom's stomach dropped suddenly as Styx changed direction, diving sharply. Tom managed to snatch a breath of air before he was plunged beneath the surface. Silty gloom met Tom as Styx dragged him

through the water. Straggly weeds
and half-decayed trunks loomed in
the murky dark.

Styx darted right, then left,
angling his body as he passed a
submerged tree, smashing Tom

against it. Jagged wood scraped
painfully down Tom's side, but he
managed to keep his grip on the
Beast. Then Styx began to roll,
turning over and over, spinning Tom
around. His head smashed against
something hard, then his shoulder
slammed into a sharp branch. He
lost his grip and tumbled from the
Beast's back, disoriented in the
filthy water. Through the churned-
up mud and slime Tom couldn't see
a thing. But he reminded himself
that the Beast wouldn't be able to
see him either. Though his lungs
were beginning to shudder for air,
he forced his body to relax. Slowly,
he sank through the dimness

towards the muddy bed of the swamp.

*You cannot hide for ever, small human*, Styx said, speaking into Tom's mind. *All who enter my realm perish, and you shall be no different*.

Tom's head was throbbing, and his chest felt like it might burst. He knew he had to take a chance and head to the surface. As slowly as he could bear to, he swam upwards, trying not to make any waves. But almost the instant he started to move, he heard the swish of the Beast's massive tail and felt the current move around him. His heart leaping with fear, Tom dived behind

a sunken tree, hoping to hide.
*SMASH!* Styx ploughed straight
through it, slamming into Tom like
a battering ram.

Blinded by pain, Tom was faintly
aware of being thrown out of the
water and into the air. He caught

a snatch
of sound
– Elenna
and Katya,
calling to
him – before
he plunged
back into
the swamp.
*BOOF!* Styx
cannoned

into his side again, crushing his ribs and driving him through the water. Stunned and winded, Tom bobbed to the surface. A faint voice in his mind was telling him he had to move. He had to get away. But his body wouldn't obey him.

*I am coming for you now!* Styx's voice rumbled. Tom tried to gather his strength, but his senses were fading, his mind starting to roam. He couldn't move.

*This is the end*, Tom thought.

# 7

# A DESPERATE ACT

Water streamed around him as he
was dragged through the swamp
by his arm. *The Beast? No.* Tom
couldn't feel teeth. His brain was
foggy with lack of air, but he
could feel the painful pressure of
something looped tightly around
his wrist like a rope... *Elenna and
Katya! They're saving me.*

But Tom could also feel the surging current of Styx closing in on him. He kicked with his legs, propelling himself forwards in a final effort to save himself. He felt mud beneath him, slowing his progress, dragging at his body, then suddenly light and air surrounded him. Tom gasped, heaving a giant breath.

"Tom!" Elenna shouted. Tom

looked over to where his friend
stood on the bank, holding the vine
that had lassoed his arm. Katya
stood behind her, holding the end of
the vine. "Watch out!"

In a rush of water, a huge cave-
like mouth opened around Tom.
Styx's javelin-sized teeth closed on
him from either side. Tom closed his
eyes, awaiting the terrible pain of
the teeth impaling him. But with a
mighty tug he was pulled from the
mouth of the Beast. He skidded on
his side through the mud. Elenna
and Katya both craned over him as
he gasped and blinked, catching his
breath, trying to focus. He saw Styx
slink back into the water.

"I thought you were gone!" Elenna said, her voice hoarse with emotion. "I thought it was your body we were pulling ashore."

"We need to get further from the water," Katya said, gazing out over the swamp. As Tom's senses cleared a little, he pushed himself up to sitting. Katya and Elenna helped him to his feet, then up the slippery bank. Every breath hurt from the pain in Tom's ribs, but he was alive. A plan began to form in his mind. He glanced between Katya and Elenna. They both looked as sodden and worn out as he felt. *It's time to end this!*

"Thank you," Tom told his friends.

"You saved my life. It was quick thinking to use a vine to pull me out, and it's given me an idea. I'm going to lure the Beast in."

"Are you sure that's such a good idea?" Katya said. "Styx almost ate you!"

Tom shrugged. "It's a desperate idea, but we have to do something. We can't leave Styx under Malvel's command. Wait here. I won't be long."

Elenna shook her head, her brow creased with worry. "Be careful!" she said. "I thought we'd lost you before. I don't want to lose you again."

"I will be!" Tom took the map from his tunic and looked for the Beast's purple marker, but Styx had vanished again. Tom reached for his red gem, hoping to get a feel for how close the Beast was.

His belt was gone.

"Styx stole my belt!" he cried. He scanned the muddy beach but there was no sign of it. "Elenna, I'll need to you to fire an arrow, to break the Beast's camouflage. Katya, be ready to follow Elenna's commands."

Taking Katya and Elenna's makeshift lasso with him, Tom waded back into the shallows. He couldn't see the Beast. But he knew that didn't mean Styx wasn't nearby.

Almost immediately, Tom felt the water of the swamp begin to stir.

Soon, waves were lapping against him, and out in the swamp, he spotted the V-shaped ripples made by the Beast. Closer and closer it came, but Tom held his ground.

"Tom, get out of there!" Elenna cried. Still, Tom didn't move...

Suddenly, with a tremendous splash, the surface broke into choppy waves and foam. Elenna's arrow whizzed past Tom. *THWACK!* Styx appeared, almost on top of Tom, his jaws open wide and Elenna's arrow lodged between his eyes. Calling on the enhanced jumping ability of his golden boots, Tom leapt high, somersaulting in the air, his magical powers propelling him high out of the water.

*Whoosh!* In a tidal wave of mud and putrid water, the Beast surged past Tom and up the bank towards Katya and Elenna. Tom righted himself in the air, then landed on the alligator's armoured back, lasso ready. Styx started to thrash and whip his head from side to side, but Tom gritted his teeth and held tight. Using the magical strength of his golden breastplate, he hooked the loop of vine around the Beast's huge snout and tugged, tightening the lasso. Tom's muscles burned as he pulled the rope tight, forcing the Beast's mouth closed. *It's working!*

Suddenly, Styx tossed his mighty head. Tom's hands, slippery and wet, lost their grip on the lasso and he was thrown off the reptile's back and into the mud. As quick as a striking snake, Styx's head whipped around, his jaws snapping open, breaking the vine. Tom scrabbled in the sludge,

clawing his way up the bank, realising he'd made a terrible mistake.

"Tom!" Elenna screamed, as the Beast

lunged, his colossal jaws closing on Tom, plunging him into foul-smelling, suffocating darkness.

Shock and disbelief held Tom frozen for a moment. *Styx has swallowed me whole!* Then fury surged inside him. *While there's blood in my veins, I will not die this way!* he vowed. Bracing his back against the roof of the Beast's mouth, Tom used his sword to prise Styx's teeth open a crack, letting in a chink of light. The stench of rotting flesh in the Beast's mouth made Tom gag. Stringy saliva covered his face and hands. *I will not die this way!* Tom repeated, thrashing his body, striving to get free.

A hideous gurgling sound came from deep within the Beast's throat, followed by a choking cough. Tom was thrown from side to side as Styx shook his head. Saliva and stinging acid bubbled up around Tom as more gurgling sounds issued from the Beast's gullet. *He's choking on me!* Tom realised. In the putrid darkness of the Beast's mouth, Tom smiled grimly. Then he kicked out with both legs, thrusting them deeper into the Beast's throat. Tom felt Styx's body spasm. *Yes!* Tom wriggled and writhed in the stringy mucus that coated Styx's insides. A blast of stinking air engulfed Tom as Styx belched. Tom retched, nausea rising inside him at the vile smell, but then kicked again, ramming his feet even further down the Beast's gullet. Another tremendous spasm wracked Styx's muscular body and a horrible gagging, heaving sound came from his gut.

Then, all at once, Styx's mouth opened, and fresh air rushed in around Tom. The Beast flopped down, limp and exhausted. Tom started to squirm his way out straight away, elbowing and clawing his way towards freedom.

"Take my hand!" Elenna called, appearing at the opening between Styx's teeth and reaching towards Tom. Katya stepped to

Elenna's side. Each grabbed one of Tom's arms and heaved. Slippery with mucus, Tom tumbled out of Styx's mouth and on to the bank. They all turned to look at the Beast. Styx was lying still, his sides heaving and his eyes half closed.

Katya pulled her axe from her belt and drew it back, ready to bury it in Styx's scales.

1

# THE POWER OF MERCY

As Katya slammed her heavy axe down towards the fallen Beast's skull, Tom blocked it with his sword.

"Hey!" Katya cried, lifting her weapon again.

Tom shook his head gravely. Something in the Beast's heavy-lidded gaze – a wretched, weary resignation – told Tom that the creature was no longer a threat. Styx was defeated.

"The Beast has fallen," Tom said. "There is no honour in striking a defenceless foe."

"But look, he's escaping!" Katya cried. Styx had heaved his immense body up out of the mud. Slowly, clumsily, the Beast half-staggered, half-slithered down the bank and slipped back into the swamp.

"I can't believe you just let him go," Katya muttered crossly.

"If we were to kill without need, we would be as bad as the Evil we battle," Elenna said.

Tom gazed out over the swamp, which was still and quiet now the Beast was gone. Suddenly, he noticed the water  swirling. Styx's blunt, scaled head broke the surface. There was something hooked around his tongue – something that glittered. *My belt!* The Beast approached the shore and deposited Tom's jewelled belt on the bank. Tom picked it up

and put it on. Setting his hand on
the ruby gem, Tom dipped his head
to the Beast.

*Thank you*, he said.

*Thank you also, Master*, Styx
replied, speaking directly into Tom's

mind. *Through your act of mercy, the Evil one's spell over me is broken. I am free.*

As Styx turned away, his outline wavered and blurred so that he became one with the water, vanishing from sight before he dipped below the surface.

Tom turned to Elenna and Katya, who were both staring after the Beast. Elenna was smiling thoughtfully, while Katya stared, open-mouthed in amazement.

"Time to send you home, Katya," Tom said. "We have two other Master of the Beasts candidates to find, and your family will be worried."

The girl shook her head fiercely. "No! Please! I'm learning so much. I can help you find the others. I want to stay and fight!"

Tom took his purple jewel from its place in his belt and wiped it clean. "You are a brave and skilful warrior," he said. "You have plenty of adventures ahead of you. But for now, the people of Tangala need to know you are safe. Take word to Prince Rotu. Tell him we will return once we have thwarted Malvel's plans."

Katya's shoulders slumped, but she nodded. "Fine," she said, then she smiled. "Once I win the Trials, I'll have plenty of chances to defeat Beasts."

Tom and Elenna smiled
too. Then Tom began to trace
a shape in the air with his
purple jewel – a large, glowing
rectangle. The jewel pulsed with
warmth, glowing brighter as Tom
finished the portal. As soon as the
shape was complete, the air within
it shimmered and a view of Rotu's
private sitting room appeared.
Compared to the dull shades of the
Netherworld, the tapestries and
paintings looked jewel-bright. Plush
cushions covered an easy chair, and
a jug of crystal-clear water stood
on a table beside a silver goblet.
Remembering his flask was almost
empty, Tom's throat ached with

longing at the sight of the clean, fresh water. But he would have to make do with refilling his flask from the swamp. He tore his eyes from the home comforts spread before him, and gestured to Katya.

"Step through, quickly," he told her. "Before the portal fails." Katya hesitated, but only for an instant.

"Goodbye," she said

to Tom and Elenna. "And good luck. I'll see you soon." Then she stepped through the portal, disappearing in a flash of silver light. Tom and Elenna were left alone once more in the gloom of the Netherworld.

"I'm glad she's safe," Elenna said. "But we have two more candidates to rescue. Time to find the next Beast, I suppose."

Tom nodded. He drew Zarlo's map from his tunic and opened it out.

"Still alive?!" Zarlo exclaimed. "Well, I must say, I'm pleasantly surprised! I thought Styx would have finished you off for sure. You might be crazy, but you're also tough, I'll give you that."

Tom and Elenna exchanged an exasperated look. "Charming!" Elenna said. "If you honestly believed an outsize lizard would get in our way, you clearly don't know us very well at all! Now, where to next?"

"Ah, now that's an excellent question," Zarlo said, an oddly gleeful tone to his voice. "I've managed to locate another Beast, and you're not going to like this one at all."

Tom shrugged, suddenly feeling energised and ready to fight. "That's never stopped us before! Let's go!"

### THE END

1

# CONGRATULATIONS, YOU HAVE COMPLETED THIS QUEST!

At the end of each chapter you were
awarded a special gold coin.
The QUEST in this book was
worth an amazing 8 coins.

Look at the Beast Quest totem picture
opposite to see how far you've come
in your journey to become

MASTER OF THE BEASTS.

The more books you read,
the more coins you will collect!

Do you want your own
Beast Quest Totem?

1. Cut out and collect the coin below
2. Go to the Beast Quest website
3. Download and print out your totem
4. Add your coin to the totem

www.beastquest.co.uk

# READ THE BOOKS, COLLECT THE COINS!
## EARN COINS FOR EVERY CHAPTER YOU READ!

**550+ COINS**
# MASTER OF THE BEASTS

550+
515
480
445

**410 COINS**
# HERO

410
395
380
365

**350 COINS**
# WARRIOR

350
320
290
260

**230 COINS**
# KNIGHT

230
217
206
191

**180 COINS**
# SQUIRE

180
146
112

**44 COINS**
# PAGE

78
44
30
19
8

**8 COINS**
# APPRENTICE

# READ ALL THE BOOKS IN SERIES 28:
## THE NETHERWORLD!

ADAM BLADE

**Beast Quest**

OSSIRON
THE FLESHLESS KILLER

ADAM BLADE

**Beast Quest**

STYX
THE LURKING TERROR

ADAM BLADE

**Beast Quest**

KAPTIVA
THE SHRIEKING SIREN

ADAM BLADE

**Beast Quest**

VELAKRO
THE LIGHTNING BIRD

*Don't miss the next exciting Beast Quest book: KAPTIVA THE SHRIEKING SIREN!*

*Read on for a sneak peek...*

# AN ILL WIND

"Wait!" Elenna said, her voice so hoarse Tom could barely hear it over the howl of the wind. He turned, glad to put his back to the constant icy blast that knifed through his clothes and hurled grit into his eyes. They had been trudging over seemingly endless mounds of black, volcanic rock beneath the dreary purple sky of the Netherworld. Under a layer of grime, Elenna's face was grey with exhaustion and covered in scratches and cuts. She took a swig from her flask, grimacing at the taste. Tom's own throat was parched, but the water they had taken from Styx's foul-smelling swamp only seemed to make him thirstier.

Tom and Elenna were on a Quest to rescue four young warriors from the clutches of Tom's oldest enemy, the Dark Wizard, Malvel. The children had been competing to become the new Master or Mistress of the Beasts for the kingdom of Tangala. Malvel had kidnapped them during the contest, transporting them to the Beast-infested wastelands of the Netherworld. The villain was now demanding that Tom give his magical purple jewel in exchange for the contestants' lives. If he got his hands on it, he'd be able to use the jewel to open a portal and escape this prison world. Tom couldn't allow that to happen.

Since crossing through Daltec's portal in search of the young heroes, Tom and Elenna had defeated two Beasts – the giant jackal, Ossiron, and the swamp monster, Styx – returning Nolan and Katya back to Tangala using the purple jewel that Malvel craved. But two more candidates, Miandra and Rafe, were still lost somewhere in the Netherworld, at the mercy of Beasts under the control of the evil sorcerer.

"Surely we have to be close to the next Beast now?" Elenna said.

"I'll check," Tom said, pulling the map of the Netherworld that Daltec had given him from his tunic.

"Still not dead, then?" a familiar, cheerful voice piped up from the parchment. It belonged to Zarlo, the ancient Avantian wizard who had created the map, only to become somehow locked inside it.

Ignoring the wizard, Tom scanned the parchment, quickly locating a small purple dot, pulsing faintly near a hastily sketched outline of a forest.

"You're only halfway through your Quest, you know?" Zarlo went on. "And already, you smell *terrible*…" The formless wizard coughed theatrically. "In fact, do you mind holding my map a bit further away?"

Elenna let out an exasperated growl. "What do you expect? We just fought a swamp monster," she said. "And how can you smell us anyway? You don't even have a nose!"

"How rude!" the wizard snapped indignantly. "I'll have you know that I–"

"Hush!" Tom hissed, holding the map close to his face so Zarlo would hear him. The wind had risen suddenly to a wild, piercing shriek. Turning to frown at the horizon, Tom spotted a dense wall of black dust, tearing towards them at impossible speed. "Elenna, look out!" he cried, just as a powerful gust slammed into him, shoving him backwards and almost snatching the map from his hands. Elenna staggered as the wind swirled around them, forcing dust into their lungs, making them both cough and choke.

Narrowing his eyes, Tom saw the dust cloud coalesce before them, swirling to become a vast, towering shape he knew only too well: a tall, hooded figure with cavernous cheeks and a cruel, skeletal grin. *Malvel!* The wizard let out a triumphant howl of laughter as Tom and Elenna bent low against the buffeting wind, fighting to keep their footing.

"That's right...*cower* before me!" Malvel boomed. "You cannot begin to imagine the power I wield! I will make you one final offer. Hand over your purple jewel, and I will return the worthless children you seek unharmed. Withhold it from me, and they shall perish in agony, far away from home!"

Tom thought of Miandra and Rafe, remembering how proudly they had stood before Prince Rotu at the start of the trials, only days before. They were both so young and filled with promise, and now they were trapped in a barren land, populated by Beasts... *I can't let them die here*, Tom thought, his hand creeping towards the purple jewel in his belt. *With the candidates safe, I could fight Malvel without risking their lives. Then I would be free to put all my focus on defeating him once and for all!*

Elenna gripped Tom's shoulder. "You can't trust Malvel," she hissed in his ear. "Do as he says, and Rafe and Miandra will be trapped here for ever."

Tom let his hand fall away from the jewel. Elenna was right. The Dark Wizard had never once kept his word in their many previous battles. Tom drew himself up against the force of the wind to stand tall. "Forget it, Malvel!" he shouted back. "We came here to defeat you, and that's what we'll do. Just as we have done every other time we've fought!"

Malvel's hideous grin vanished. His hollow eyes narrowed with hatred. "Then they shall die here in the Netherworld!" he cried. "And so shall you. I am more than happy to wait while you starve in this wilderness. I'll be more than happy to prise the jewel from the rotting remains of your corpse." With a deafening howl of wind, the wizard's shadowy form dissolved into eddying tendrils of dust.

Read
*KAPTIVA THE SHRIEKING SIREN*
to find out what happens next!